Windy Nights

and Other Poems

Contents

Windy Nights

Whenever the moon and stars are set,
    Whenever the wind is high,
All night long in the dark and wet,
    A man goes riding by.
Late in the night when the fires are out,
Why does he gallop and gallop about?

Whenever the trees are crying aloud,
    And ships are tossed at sea,
By, on the highway, low and loud,
    By at the gallop goes he.
By at the gallop he goes, and then
By he comes back at the gallop again.

Robert Louis Stevenson

Snowsheeting

When winter comes, it's freezing cold,
and we know where to go.
We all pile into Dad's old car, and head off for the snow.
We grab our woollen mittens, and our hats and beanies, too,
And our heavy, padded parkas,
to warm us through and through.

We do not own toboggans, no snowboards and no skis,
But still we have a lot of fun. We have no need of these.
Yes, we have something special that is very hard to beat.
Folded in the car boot is our great big plastic sheet.

We don't go to a large resort that's very far away.
We choose a smaller, closer hill, and go there for the day.
We park the car and grab the sheet,
and head towards the snow.

We make a little snowman, and there's snowballs, too,
to throw.

And so we take it turn by turn, clomping to the hill,
Then sliding to the bottom on our plastic – what a thrill!
Snow slops down inside my shirt. It drops into my boots.
It's up my sleeve and down my pants,
but I don't give two hoots!

I'm climbing, climbing, climbing,
and I'm sweating with the heat,
Then I'm sliding, sliding, sliding
on our mighty slippery sheet.
We take a break to get the thermos – hot tomato soup,
And homemade cake and sandwiches
to feed the starving troop.

At last, alas, the time arrives that homeward we must drive.
What a mighty day it's been! It's great to be alive!
It's very dark outside the car, as home again we creep,
But long before we reach our door, we kids are fast asleep!

Stephen Whiteside

The Flood

Well, it rained five days
        and the sky was as dark as night.
Yes, it rained five days
        and the sky was as dark as night.
There's trouble in the lowlands tonight.

I got up one morning.
        I couldn't even get out of my door,
I got up one morning.
        I couldn't even get out of my door,
That was enough trouble to make a poor boy
        wonder where to go.

I went and stood up on a high lonesome hill,
I went and stood up on a high lonesome hill,
I did all I could to look down
on the house where I used to live.
It thundered and it lightninged
and the wind began to blow.
It thundered and it lightninged
and the wind began to blow.
There were thousands of poor people
didn't have no place to go.

Anonymous

My Bike

Dusk
wind whistles in my ears
smooth path
tyres hum
swooping through the gardens
no hands
sending the possums jumping for the trees
tailwind
I'm flying!

Elizabeth Honey

Waking Up

Oh! I have just had such a lovely dream!
And then I woke,
And all the dream went out like kettle-steam,
Or chimney-smoke.

My dream was all about – how funny, though!
I've only just
Dreamed it, and now it has begun to blow
Away like dust.

In it I went – no! in my dream I had –
No, that's not it!
I can't remember, oh, it is too *bad,*
My dream a bit.

But I saw something beautiful, I'm sure –
Then someone spoke,
And then I didn't see it any more,
Because I woke.

Eleanor Farjeon

The Underground Train

Once you get on the underground train
The people stare at you.
Their eyes
seem to be glued on you
From the moment you get on the train
until the moment you get off the train
Their eyes look like bronze
No one speaks
They all stay quiet and still

You try to stop looking at them
But you can't
Then some of them look up
At the posters on the roof
But they soon stare back at you again.
The train stops
Suddenly there is a buzz of conversation
At last you are out
You feel much better.

Jayne Spooner

Building a Skyscraper

They're building a skyscraper
Near our street.
Its height will be nearly
One thousand feet.

It covers completely
A city block.
They drilled its foundation
Through solid rock.

They made its framework
Of great steel beams
With riveted joints
And welded seams.

A swarm of workmen
Strain and strive
Like busy bees
In a honeyed hive.

Building the skyscraper
Into the air
While crowds of people
Stand and stare.

James S. Tippett

The Eagle

He clasps the crag with crooked hands;
Close to the sun in lonely lands,
Ring'd with the azure world, he stands.

The wrinkled sea beneath him crawls;
He watches from his mountain walls,
And like a thunderbolt he falls.

Alfred, Lord Tennyson

The Duck

Behold the duck.
It does not cluck.
A cluck it lacks.
It quacks.
It is specially fond
Of a puddle or pond.
When it dines or sups,
It bottom ups.

Ogden Nash

The Cow

The friendly cow all red and white,
I love with all my heart:
She gave me cream with all her might.
To eat with apple-tart.

She wanders lowing here and there,
And yet she cannot stray,
All in the pleasant open air,
The pleasant light of day;

And blown by all the winds that pass
And wet with all the showers,
She walks among the meadow grass
And eats the meadow flowers.

Robert Louis Stevenson

Meems

Other cats purr
and so does Meems.

Other cats creep
and so does Meems.

Other cats sleep
and so does Meems,

But Meems
dreams.

She dreams of moths with velvet wings.
She dreams of prawns (her favourite things).
She dreams of windows striped with rain
and dipping her nose in a puddle again.

Other cats miaow, other cats snore,
other cats lie in a slope on the floor
but Meems

dreams.

Adèle Geras

The Triantiwontigongolope

There's a very funny insect that you do not often spy,
And it isn't quite a spider, and it isn't quite a fly;
It is something like a beetle, and a little like a bee,
But nothing like a woolly grub that climbs upon a tree.
Its name is quite a hard one, but you'll learn it soon, I hope.
So try:
    Tri-
        Tri-anti-wonti-
            Triantiwontigongolope.

It lives on weeds and wattle-gum, and has a funny face;
Its appetite is hearty, and its manner a disgrace.
When first you come upon it, it will give you quite a scare,
But when you look for it again, you find it isn't there.
And unless you call it softly it will stay away and mope.
So try:
    Tri-
        Tri-anti-wonti-
            Triantiwontigongolope.

It trembles if you tickle it or tread upon its toes;
It is not an early riser, but it has a snubbish nose.
If you sneer at it, or scold it, it will scuttle off in shame,
But it purrs and purrs quite proudly if you call it by its name,
And offer it some sandwiches of sealing-wax and soap.
So try:
    Tri-
        Tri-anti-wonti-
            Triantiwontigongolope.

But of course you haven't seen it; and I truthfully confess
That I haven't seen it either, and I don't know its address.
For there isn't such an insect,
though there really might have been
If the trees and grass were purple,
and the sky was bottle-green.
It's just a joke of mine, which you'll forgive, I hope.
Oh, try!
Tri-
Tri-anti-wonti-
Triantiwontigongolope.

CJ Dennis

If Pigs Could Fly

If pigs could fly, I'd fly a pig
To foreign countries small and big –
To Italy and Spain,
To Austria, where cowbells ring,
To Germany, where people sing –
And then come home again.

I'd see the Ganges and the Nile;
I'd visit Madagascar's isle,
And Persia and Peru.
People would say they'd never seen
So odd, so strange an air-machine
As that on which I flew.

Why everyone would raise a shout
To see his trotters and his snout
Come floating from the sky;
And I would be a famous star
Well known in countries near and far –
If only pigs could fly!

James Reeves

Windy Nights and Other Poems

Text: Various
Series consultant: Annette Smith
Publishing editor: Simone Calderwood
Editor: Annabel Smith
Designer: Karen Mayo
Series designers: James Lowe and Karen Mayo
Illustrations: Gregory Baldwin, Tracie Grimwood and Mark Guthrie
Permissions: Helen Mammides
Production controller: Erin Dowling
Reprint: Siew Han Ong

PM Guided Reading

Silver Level 24

The Indoor Forest
The Troublesome Terrarium
Aeroplanes
Heavy Machines
The Mysterious Time Capsule
Sleeping Beauty: A Modern Tale
Animals with Armour
Outdoor Art Activities
Windy Nights and Other Poems
Our Brother Andy

ISBN 978 0 17 036590 1

Cengage Learning Australia
Level 5 , 80 Dorcas Street
Southbank VIC 3006
Phone: 1300 790 853
Email: aust.nelsonprimary@cengage.com

For learning solutions, visit cengage.com.au

Acknowledgements
We would like to thank and acknowledge the following for permission to reproduce copyright material:

Windy Nights and The Cow, by Robert Louis Stevenson; Snowsheeting, by Stephen Whiteside, from The Billy that Died with His Boots On, Walker Books, 2014; The Flood, Anonymous, adapted from the song 'Backwater Blues' by Bessie Smith (1894-1937); My Bike, by Elizabeth Honey, from Mongrel Doggerel, Allen & Unwin, 1998; Waking Up, by Eleanor Farjeon, from Silver Sand and Snow, Michael Joseph, 1951, reproduced with permission by David Higham; The Underground Train, by Jayne Spooner; Building a Skyscraper, by James S. Tippett, from A World to Know, Harper & Brothers Publishers 1933, used by permission of Harper Collins Publishers; The Eagle, by Alfred, Lord Tennyson; The Duck, by Ogden Nash, from 'Barnyard Cogitations', in the June 6, 1936 issue of The Saturday Evening Post, licensed by Curtis Licensing, Indianapolis IN.; Meems, © Adele Geras; The Triantiwontigongolope, by CJ Dennis, from A Book for Kids, Angus & Robertson, 1921; If Pigs Could Fly, © James Reeves, from The Complete Poems for Children, Faber Finds, 2011.

Every effort has been made to trace and acknowledge copyright. However, if any infringement has occurred, the publishers tender their apologies and invite the copyright holders to contact them.

Printed in China by 1010 Printing International Ltd
13 25

This product is made from materials that are compliant with the EU Deforestation Regulation

15
16
17
18
19
20
21
22
23
PM Level 24
25
26
27
28
29
30

A mysterious man galloping on a horse all night, a boy at the top of a hill by moonlight ... Waking up from weird and wonderful dreams, and a curious, sleepy cat called Meems!

Read about all these things and more in this collection of poems.

Text Type:
Poetry (Imaginative)

Dancing in Water

Story by Diana Noonan

Illustrations by Nathalie Ortega

PM

Dancing in Water

Level 21

Running Words 671 **Text Type** Narrative

Curriculum Areas English (Literacy, Literature, Language); The Arts (Dance); Health and Physical Education

Retelling to Encourage Critical Thinking About the Content

Ask each student to retell the story in their own words.

Record the retelling for further discussion and reflection.

Questions to Reinforce Meaning and Stimulate Discussion

Literal

1 What was one of the things that Skylar liked about dancing?

2 What did Skylar use to help her hold her breath underwater?

3 What did Skylar learn to do when she tried out for the artistic swimming team?

Inferential

4 Why did Skylar gasp when Dr Lei said she needed a year's rest from dancing?

5 Why do you think Skylar liked the girls' colourful swimming costumes?

6 Do you think Skylar has seen artistic swimming before? Why?

7 Why did Rachel ask Skylar if she had ever been to dance class?

8 Why did Skylar worry about getting into the artistic swimming team?

Applied Knowledge

9 How is artistic swimming similar to dancing?

10 Why is Skylar able to 'dance in water' but no longer able to do ballet dancing?

Links with Other PM Guided Reading Books

Level 21	Narrative	*The Glass Bead Bracelet*
Level 21	Information Report	*Outdoor Adventure Parks*
Level 21	Information Report	*Olympic Cycling*
Level 22	Narrative	*Arlo's Skatepark Surprise*